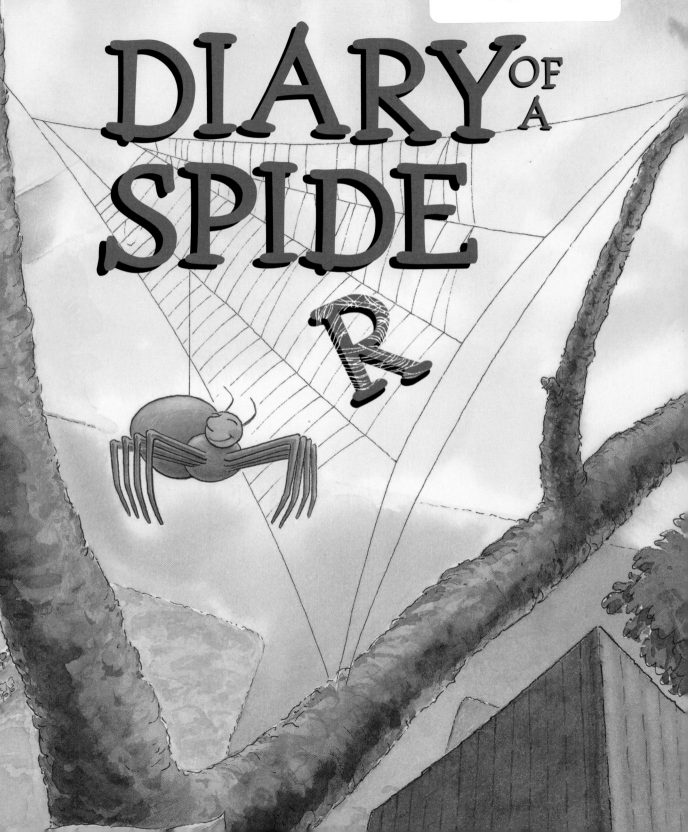

DIARY OF A SPIDER

Family portrait

Cool, huh?

Discovered this neat sculpture!

Fly's little sister, Maggot

My first web

My favorite book, *Charlotte's Web*

Baby picture of me and Grampa

For the girls—
Meghan, Jacqueline, Theresa,
Kerry, and Amanda
—D.C.

For Valerie
—H.B.

ISBN 978-0-545-24330-8

Text copyright © 2005 by Doreen Cronin. Illustrations copyright © 2005 by Harry Bliss.
All rights reserved. Published by Scholastic Inc., 557 Broadway, New York, NY 10012,
by arrangement with HarperCollins Children's Books, a division of HarperCollins
Publishers. SCHOLASTIC and associated logos are trademarks and/or registered
trademarks of Scholastic Inc.

12 11 10 9 8 7 6 5 4 3 2 1   11 12 13 14 15 16/0

Printed in the U.S.A.   40

First Scholastic paperback printing, January 2011

Typography by Alicia Mikles

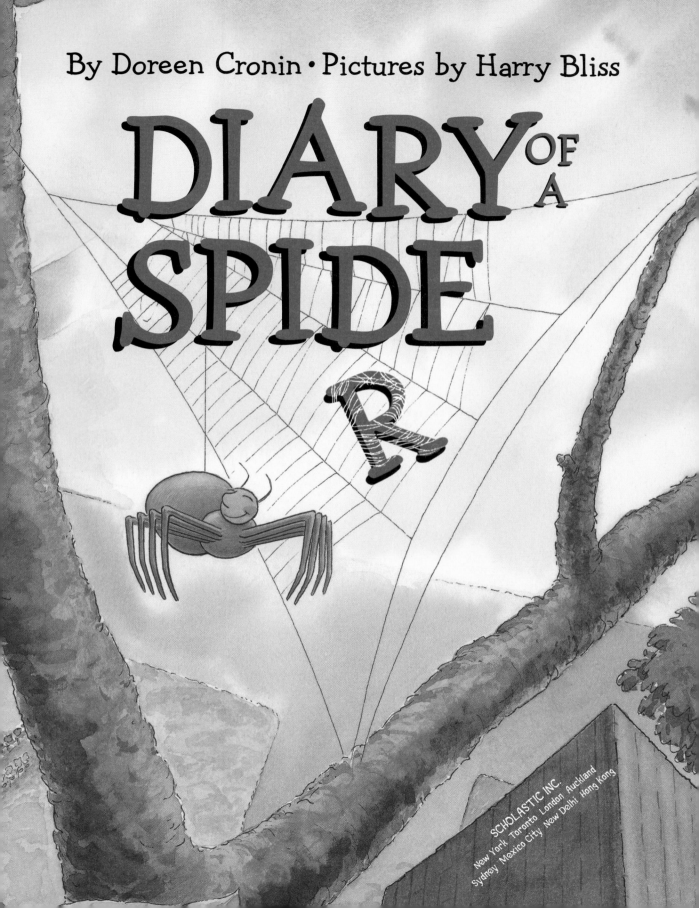

By Doreen Cronin • Pictures by Harry Bliss

DIARY OF A SPIDER

SCHOLASTIC INC.
New York Toronto London Auckland
Sydney Mexico City New Delhi Hong Kong

MARCH 1

Today was Grandparents Day at
school, so I brought Grampa with me.

He taught us three things:

1. Spiders are not insects—insects
have six legs.

INSECTS | SPIDERS

2. Without spiders, insects could take over the world.

3. Butterflies taste better with a little barbecue sauce.

MARCH 16

Grampa says that in his day, flies
and spiders did not get along.

MARCH 29

Today in gym class we learned how to catch the wind so we could travel to faraway places.

When I got home, I made up
flash cards so I could practice:

2.
Release
silk.

1.
Climb
high.

3.
Catch
wind.

Fly made up her own flash card:

1.
Fly.

I'm starting to
see why Grampa
doesn't like her.

APRIL 1

Went to the park with my sister today.
We tried the seesaw.

It didn't work.

We tried the tire swing.

It didn't work.

We spun a huge sticky web
on the water fountain.

That worked.

EEEEEEK!

APRIL 12

Today was Safety Day at school. We
learned that vacuums eat spiderwebs
and are very, very dangerous.
If we hear a vacuum,
we should Stop,
Drop, and Run.

STOP WHAT
WE'RE DOING.
DROP FROM
THE WEB.
RUN LIKE
CRAZY.

PARTY
CANDLES
40 CT

CANDLES

APRIL 13

We had a vacuum drill today.
I stopped what I was doing.

Forgot where I was going.

And ran screaming from the room.

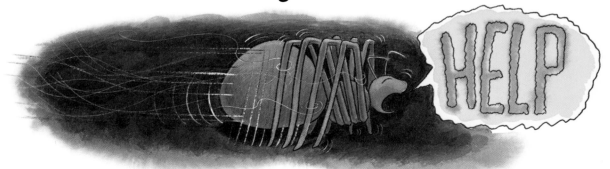

We're having another drill tomorrow.

APRIL 17

I'm sleeping over at Worm's house tonight.

I hope they don't have leaves and rotten tomatoes for dinner again.

Today was show-and-tell.
So I brought in my old skin.

My teacher called on it to
lead the Pledge of Allegiance.

Daddy Longlegs made fun of Fly
because she eats with her feet.
Now she won't come out of her
tree house.

I'm going to find him and give him a piece of my mind!

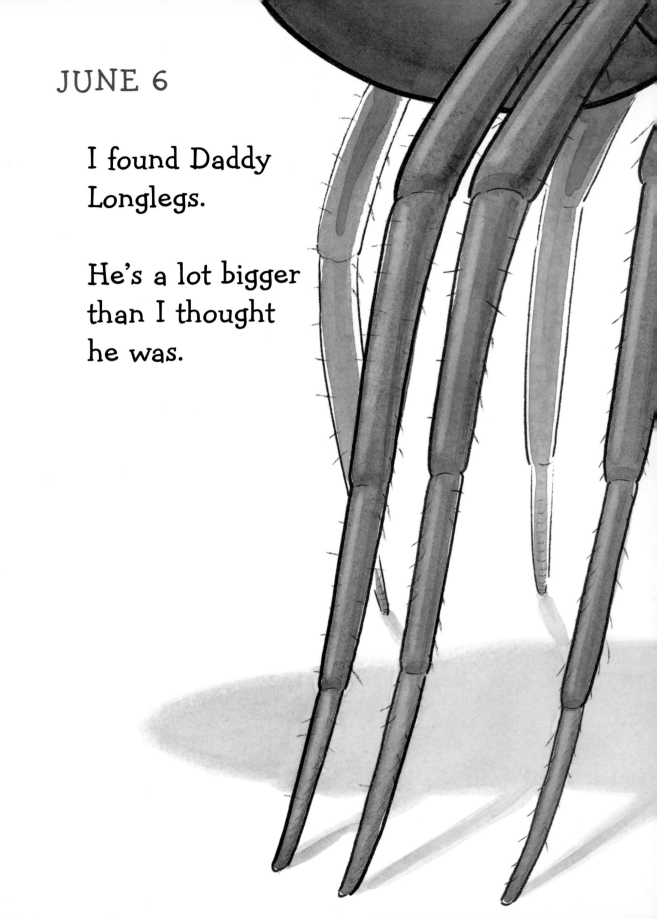

JUNE 6

I found Daddy
Longlegs.

He's a lot bigger
than I thought
he was.

I gave him a piece
of my lunch
instead.

Fly's tree house blew away
in the wind today.

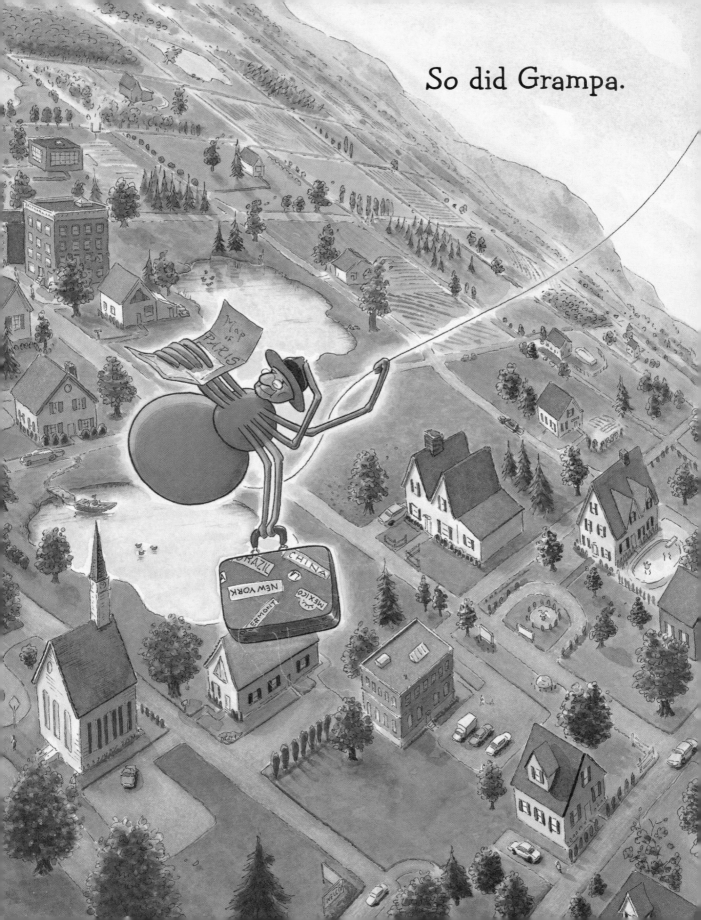

So did Grampa.

JUNE 18

I got a postcard from Grampa today:

PARIS – FRANCE

Dear Spider,
Ooh-la-la!
I landed in Paris!
French bugs are
delicious!
Au revoir,
Grampa

leg → of French gnat... give it a try!

Spider
5 Web Ave.
Arachnidville
05400
USA

Tarет CO.

Grampa came home today.

I couldn't wait to hear about
how he rode the winds
all the way over the ocean!

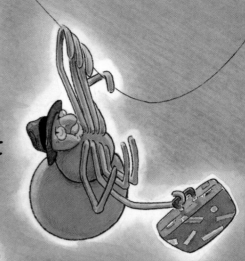

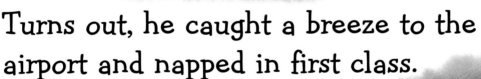

Turns out, he caught a breeze to the
airport and napped in first class.

JULY 2

Fly came over to play today. She got stuck in
our web, and her mom had to come get her.

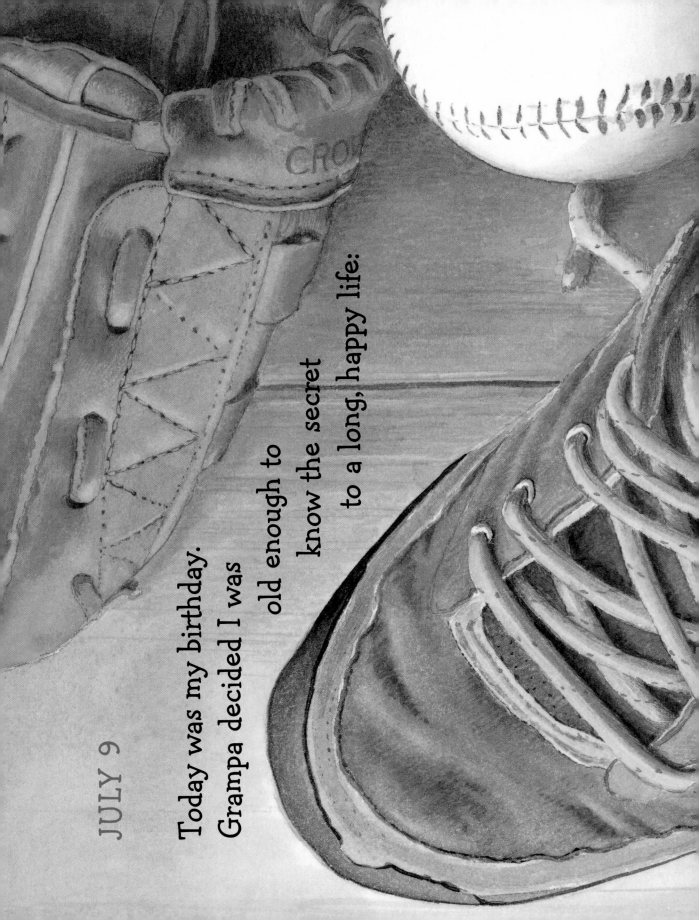

JULY 9

Today was my birthday.
Grampa decided I was
old enough to
know the secret
to a long, happy life:

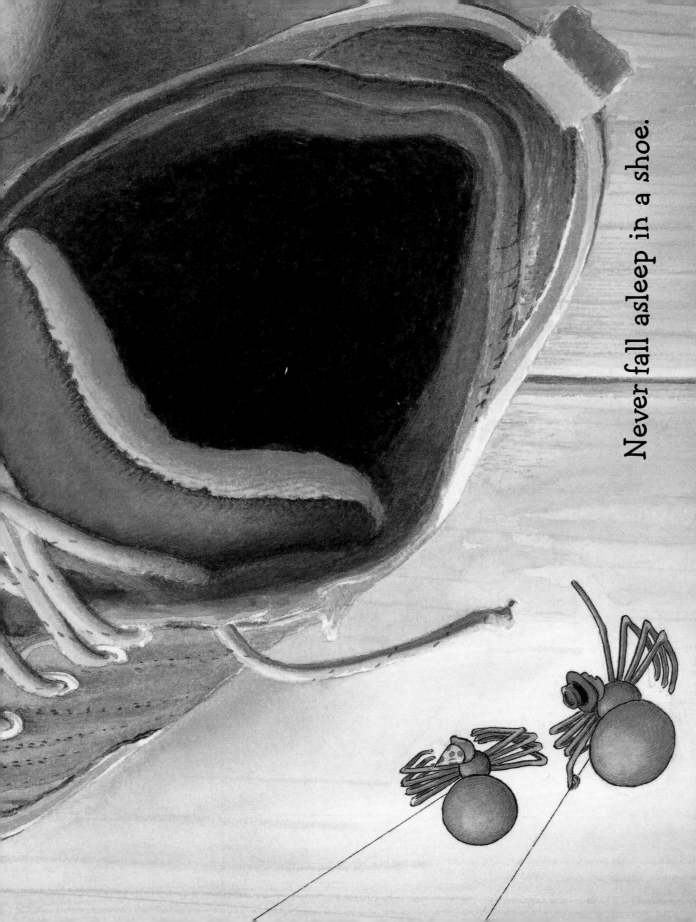

Never fall asleep in a shoe.

JULY 16

Things I scare:

1. Fly's mom

2. Tiny bugs

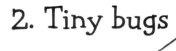

3. People using water fountains at the park

JULY 17

Things that scare me:

1. Daddy Longlegs

2. Vacuums

3. People with big feet

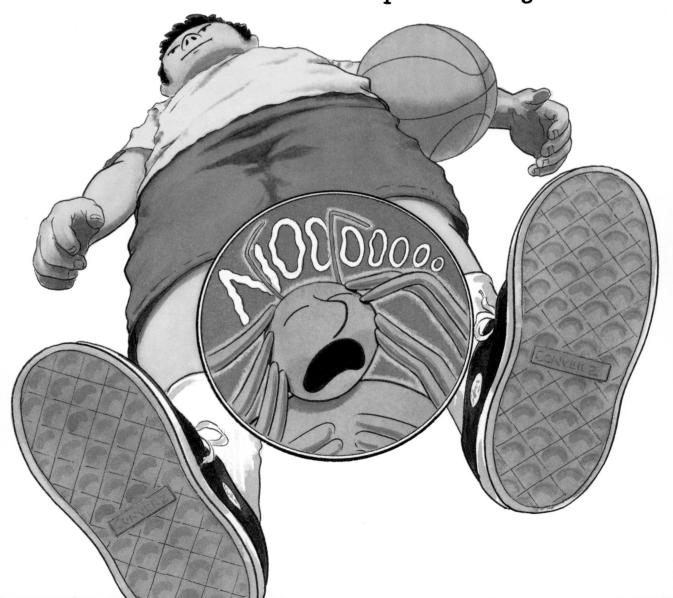

AUGUST 1

I wish that people wouldn't judge all spiders based on the few spiders that bite.

I know if we took the time to get to know each other, we would get along just fine.

Just like me and Fly.

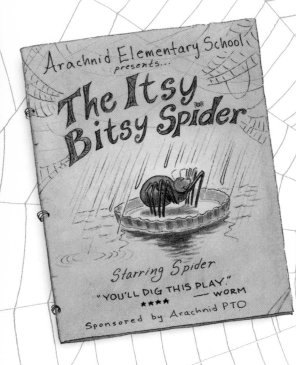

Dad made me this!

Worm found this!

My best friends

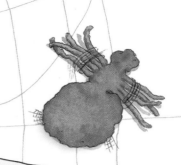

My first molted skin

Extended family reunion

I made this slingshot!